W9-BKE-008

1/12

Delta County Libraries

PO BOX 858
Delta, CO 81416
www.deltalibraries.org

The Family Storybook
TREASURY

TALES *of* LAUGHTER, CURIOSITY, *and* FUN

Delta County Libraries

PO BOX 858
Delta, CO 81416
www.deltalibraries.org

Houghton Mifflin Harcourt
Boston New York 2011

*W*hile reading together is always a wonderful way to spend loving, fun-filled family time, there are some stories and poems that are a special joy to share. These are the ones that come down off the bookshelf again and again—and show the signs of the love showered on them. Collected in this book are eight picture books and eight poems that are brimming with memorable characters, hilarious situations, remarkable writing, and stunning illustrations from world-renowned artists.

So, open the pages of this treasury with a child you love, and share the timeless tales and modern classics within them—and discover the old friends and new acquaintances gathered here, together.

Contents

MARGRET & H. A. REY'S

Curious George
and the Firefighters

Illustrated in the style of H. A. Rey by Anna Grossnickle Hines

This is George.

He was a good little monkey and always very curious.

Today George and his friend the man with the yellow hat joined
Mrs. Gray and her class on their field trip to the fire station.

The Fire Chief was waiting for them right next to a big red fire truck. "Welcome!" he said, and he led everyone upstairs to begin their tour.

There was a kitchen with a big table, and there were snacks for everyone. The Fire Chief told them all about being a firefighter. George tried hard to pay attention, but there were so many things for a little monkey to explore. Like that shiny silver pole in the corner . . .

Where did that pole go? George was curious.

Why, it went back downstairs! There was the
great big fire truck. There was a map of the city.
And there was a whole wall full of coats and hats
and big black boots!

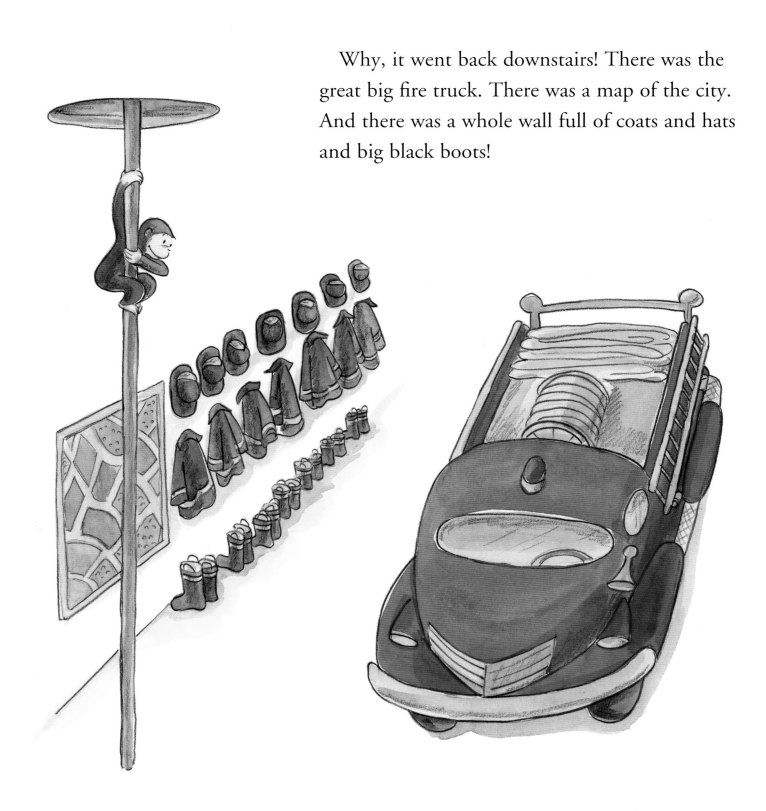

George had an idea.
First he stepped into a
pair of boots.

Next, he picked out a helmet.

And, finally, George put on a jacket.
He was a firefighter!

Suddenly . . . *BRRRIINNGG!*

The firefighters all rushed in.

"This is not my helmet!" said one.

"My boots are too big!" said another.

"Hurry! Hurry!" called the Fire Chief. A bright red light on the map of the city told him just where the fire was. There was no time to waste!

One by one, the firefighters jumped into the fire truck.

And so did George.

The fire truck with all the firefighters sped out of the firehouse.
And so did George!
The siren screamed and the lights flashed.

The truck turned right. Then it turned left.
WHOO WHOO WHOO went the whistle, and George held on tight.

And just like that the fire truck and all the firefighters pulled up to a pizza parlor on Main Street. Smoke was coming out of a window in the back and a crowd was gathering in the street.

"Thank goodness you're here!" cried the cook.

The firefighters rushed off the truck and started
unwinding their hoses. They knew just what to do.
And George was ready to help.
He climbed up on the hose reel . . .

One of the firefighters saw George trying to help, and he took George by the arm and led him out of the way.

"A fire is no place for a monkey!" he said to George. "You stay here where it's safe."

George felt terrible.

George sat on the bench and looked around. Next to him on the ground was a bucket full of balls. George reached in and took one out. It fit in his hand just right, like the apple he'd had for a snack.

A little girl was watching George. He tried to give her the ball, but she was too frightened.

George took another ball.
And another.

"Look," a boy said. "That monkey is juggling!"

The boy took a ball from the bucket and tossed it to George, but it went too high.

George climbed up onto the fire truck to get it.

Now George had four balls to juggle. He threw the balls higher and higher. He juggled with his hands. He juggled with his feet. He could do all kinds of tricks!

The boy threw another ball to George. George threw the ball back to the boy. The little girl reached down and picked up a ball, too. Soon all the children were throwing and catching, back and forth.

The Fire Chief came to tell everyone that the fire was out. Just then, the little girl laughed and said, "Look, Mommy—a fire monkey!"

"Hey!" called the Fire Chief. "What are you doing up there?"

"What a wonderful idea," the little girl's mother said to the Fire Chief. "Bringing this brave little monkey to help children when they're frightened."

"Oh," the Fire Chief said. "Well, er, thank you."

Before long the fire truck was back at the fire house, where a familiar voice called, "George!" It was the man with the yellow hat.

"This little monkey had quite an adventure," said one of the firefighters.

"Is everyone all right?" asked Mrs. Gray.

"Yes, it was just a small fire," said the Fire Chief.
"And George was a big help."
Now the field trip was coming to an end.
But there was one more treat in store . . .

All the children got to take a ride around the neighborhood on the shiny red fire truck, and they each got their very own fire helmet. Even George! And it was just the right size for a brave little monkey.

The Cheetah

The cheetah is *fleet*.
The cheetah is *fast*.
Its four furry feet
Have already passed.

by Douglas Florian

Lyle Walks the Dogs

A COUNTING BOOK

By BERNARD WABER   Illustrated by PAULIS WABER

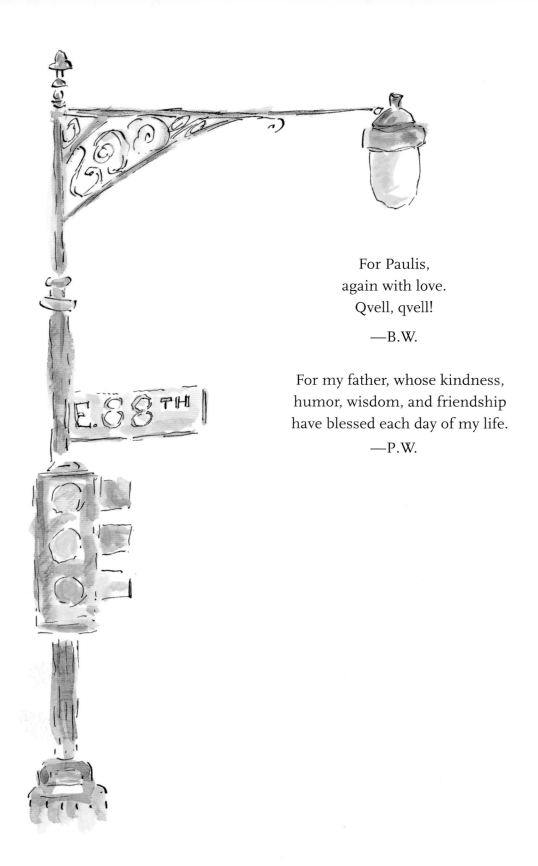

For Paulis,
again with love.
Qvell, qvell!

—B.W.

For my father, whose kindness,
humor, wisdom, and friendship
have blessed each day of my life.

—P.W.

Lyle the Crocodile has a job, a brand-new job.

Lyle's job is walking dogs.

It is a very good job for Lyle because Lyle loves dogs.

And he loves to walk.

And best of all, Lyle loves being helpful to others.

Lyle is so happy. Today is Day 1, the first day of his job.

DAY 1

GWENDOLYN

Lyle walks **1** dog.

The dog's name is Gwendolyn.

Uh-oh! Gwendolyn is frisky.

She pulls this way and she pulls that way.

Lyle must take quick skipping steps to keep up with Gwendolyn.

No problem. Lyle loves skipping.

DAY 2

Lyle walks **2** dogs.

Count them—**1-2**. The second dog's name is Morris.

Oh . . . and guess what?

Morris is even friskier.

Lyle must take even quicker steps to keep up
with Morris.

No more skipping. Too bad!

MORRIS

33

3

POKEY

DAY 3

Lyle walks **3** dogs.

Count them—**1-2-3.**

The third dog's name is Pokey.

Pokey takes his own good,

sweet time walking.

Slow down, Morris!
Slow down, Gwendolyn!
Come along, Pokey!
Good going, Pokey.
Good work, Lyle.

4
FRISKY

DAY 4

Lyle walks **4** dogs.

Count them—**1-2-3-4**.

The fourth dog's name is . . .

oh, no! Her name is Frisky.

Hang on to Frisky, Lyle!

DAY 5

Lyle walks **5** dogs.

Count them—**1-2-3-4-5**.

The fifth dog's name is Rosie.

Rosie loves birds, bugs, flowers, children—
and Lyle. Most certainly Lyle.

ROSIE

5

6

SNAPPY

DAY 6

Business is picking up.

Lyle walks **6** dogs.

Count them—**1-2-3-4-5-6**.

The sixth dog's name is Snappy.

Snappy is . . . well . . . rather snappish.

He barks and barks. And barking, as you know,

can be quite contagious, especially for dogs.

Six dogs barking. What a racket! What to do?

Leave it to Lyle.

His gentle tugs, pats, and shushes calm everyone—

even snappish Snappy.

7

TULIP

DAY 7

Lyle's excellent reputation for walking dogs has spread.
Lyle walks **7** dogs. Count them—**1-2-3-4-5-6-7.**
The seventh dog's name is Tulip.
Tulip had to be coaxed out from under the couch.
Everyone waited and waited for her.

But now look at Tulip.
Just look at her trotting along,
merrily wagging her tail with the best of them.

8

SCRAPPY

DAY 8

Lyle walks **8** dogs.

Count them—**1-2-3-4-5-6-7-8.**

The eighth dog's name is Scrappy.

Scrappy runs, stops, or sits as he

chooses to run, stop . . .

. . . or sit.

There's trouble on East 88th Street.

Not to worry. Lyle is on the job.

His kind heart and big croc smile win the day.

Scrappy falls quickly in step,

and all step cheerfully together.

Big cheers for Lyle.

43

RUFUS

9

DAY 9

Lyle walks **9** dogs.

Count them—**1-2-3-4-5-6-7-8-9.**

The ninth dog's name is Rufus.

Rufus is so happy to be walking with Lyle.

He scratched at his window for days, yearning
to join the walk.

And Lyle is tickled to have Rufus aboard.

10

SNIFFY

DAY 10

Lyle walks **10** dogs.

Count them—**1-2-3-4-5-6-7-8-9-10.**

The tenth dog's name is Sniffy.

Sniffy walks nose to the ground,

sniffing, sniffing, sniffing.

Suddenly, Sniffy is on to something.

What?

A SQUIRREL!

The dogs run.
The squirrel runs.
Lyle runs, too.

Are all of the dogs here?

Let's count them and see.

1

GWENDOLYN

2

MORRIS

3

POKEY

7

TULIP

8

SCRAPPY

9

RUFUS

4

FRISKY

5

ROSIE

6

SNAPPY

10

SNIFFY

They are all here.

Safe, well—and thirsty.
Good dogs!

And—

Good job, Lyle!

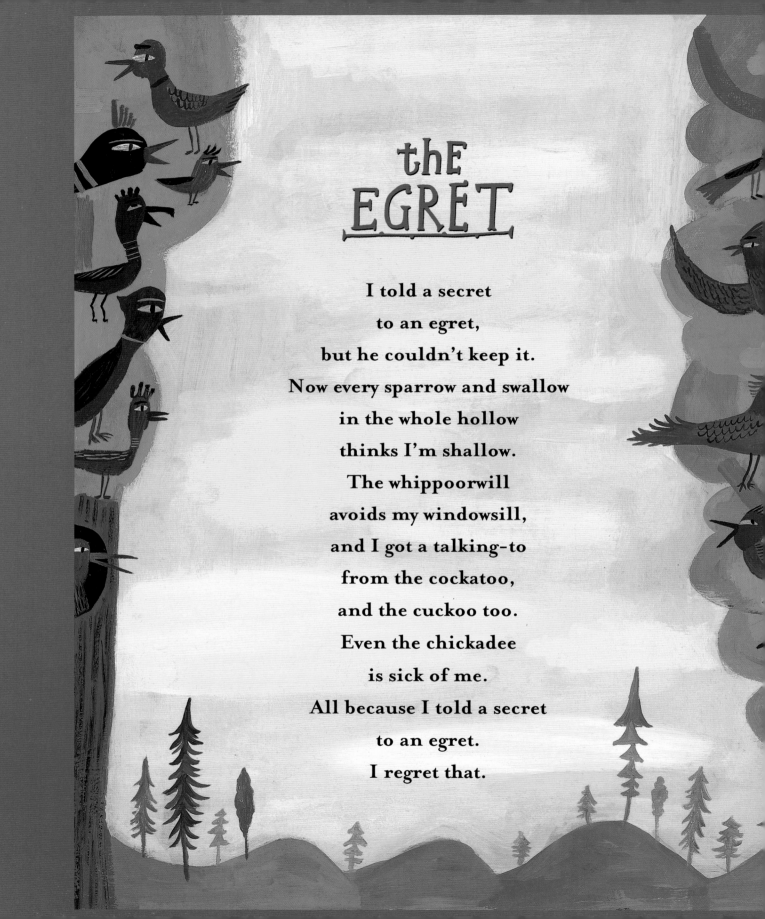

tHE EGRET

I told a secret
to an egret,
but he couldn't keep it.
Now every sparrow and swallow
in the whole hollow
thinks I'm shallow.
The whippoorwill
avoids my windowsill,
and I got a talking-to
from the cockatoo,
and the cuckoo too.
Even the chickadee
is sick of me.
All because I told a secret
to an egret.
I regret that.

by Calef Brown

SUSAN MEDDAUGH

For the Finneys

The day Helen gave Martha dog her alphabet soup,

something unusual happened.

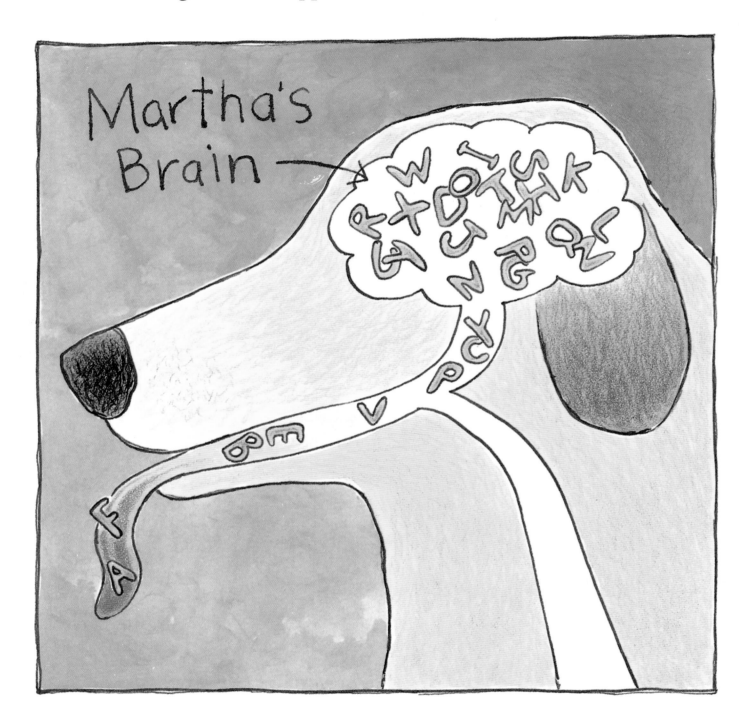

The letters in the soup went up to Martha's brain
instead of down to her stomach.

That evening, Martha spoke.

Martha's family had many questions to ask her.
Of course, she had a lot to tell them!

62

Alphabet soup became a regular part of Martha's diet, and the family had a wonderful time surprising people. Walking the dog was always good for a laugh.

They ordered pizza from a different restaurant every night.

They taught Martha how to use the phone.

But this was a mistake.

Pretty soon, more than pizza was being delivered!

Family and friends were amazed.

Although there were those who doubted,

Martha always had the last word.

But there was a problem:
now that Martha could talk, there was no stopping her.
She said exactly what was on her mind.

She made embarrassing comments.

And, she always told the truth.

Occasionally she wondered why
her family was often mad at her.

71

But she kept on talking.
She talked through everyone's favorite TV shows,

except her own.

She talked while they were trying to read.

73

She talked and talked...

I was born in a back alley to a poor but loving mother. Although she was a mixed breed, Momma was determined to raise us puppies right, to give us a solid background before we went out into the world at eight weeks. Even before our eyes were open, Momma would say: "You're dogs! Not cats! Don't ever forget that!" Blah Blah Blah Blah Bla Blah Blah Blah

I still remember the rules Momma gave us to live by: ① Beware of Two-year-old humans with clothes-pins. ② Under the table is the very best place to be during a meal. ③ Never mistake your human's leg for a tree.

...Blah... Blah Blah... Blah Blah Blah (that was for my brothers, of course.) And...

④ if it's black and white and smells funny, it's not a cat. Don't chase it.

Blah Blah Blah Blah Blah Blah Blah Blah

And while we're on the subject, I understand Cat, but I can't speak it. Blah Bla

Wait... where was I? Blah

Oh yes.... Blah

Blah Blah Blah

and talked…

until her family could not stand it and said, "Martha, *please!*"

"What's wrong?" asked Martha.
"You talk too much!" yelled Father.
"You never stop!" yelled Mother.
"Sometimes," said Helen,
"I wish you had never learned to talk."

Martha was crushed.

The next day, Martha did not speak. She didn't ask
for her dinner, or to go out. She offered no opinions,
but lay quietly beneath the kitchen table.

At first her family enjoyed the silence, but after
a while they became worried.
"What's the matter, Martha?" asked Helen.
Martha didn't answer.
Helen's father called the vet.
"There's something wrong with my dog!" he sad.
"She won't say a word."
"Is this some kind of a joke?" snapped the vet.

Helen offered Martha bowl after bowl of alphabet soup,
but Martha had lost her appetite for letters.

Martha's family wondered if she would ever speak again.

Then one evening when her family was out, Martha heard the sound of glass breaking.

"A burglar!" she gasped. "I better call the police."

She carefully dialed 911.

But when she opened her mouth to speak—

Martha hadn't eaten a bowl of alphabet soup in days!

Martha raced to the kitchen.
She barked. She growled.
She tried to look ferocious.

The burglar wasn't frightened. He picked up a pot
from the stove.

"Uh, oh," thought Martha. "It's taps for sure."
But to her surprise, the burglar put the pot down
on the floor in front of her.
"Here, doggy," he said. "Have something nice to eat."

The burglar smiled as he closed Martha into the kitchen
and went back to work.

"Dumb dog," he said.
"Lucky for me you like alphabet soup."

When Martha's family returned, they found the police removing the burglar from their house.

"How did you know he was robbing our house?" asked Helen.

"We got a call at the station," said the officer.

"Some lady named Martha."

"Good dog, Martha!" exclaimed her happy family.
"You're so right," said Martha.

Now Martha eats a bowl of alphabet soup every day.
She's learning what to say and when to say it, and
sometimes she doesn't say anything at all . . .
at least for a few minutes.

CATERPILLAR

The word wriggles in my pocket.
CATERPILLAR.
I reach for it, but it worms away
crawling fast as it can. I get down
on my hands and knees and chase it.

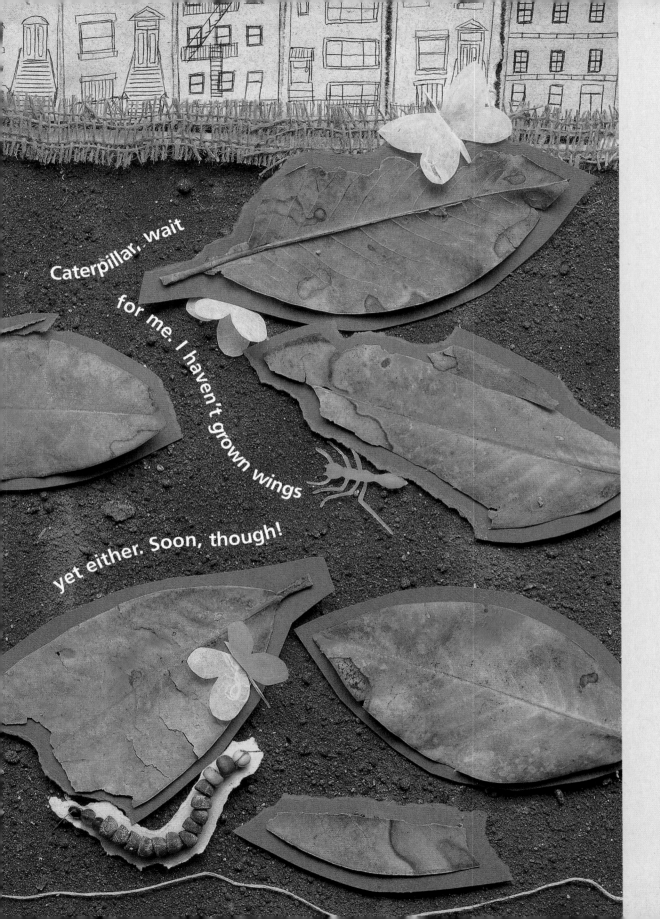

Caterpillar, wait
for me. I haven't grown wings
yet either. Soon, though!

by Nikki Grimes
illustrated by Javaka Steptoe

The Great Doughnut Parade

Written and illustrated by

Rebecca Bond

The great parade began with a doughnut
that Billy had tied to his belt with a string.

The doughnut brought Hen, with a *cluck! cluck! cluck!*

She fancied herself a crumb of this thing.

And then came Cat, all quiet and slinky

and now Big Dog with a bounce like a spring,

together all racing and chasing one doughnut

that Billy had tied to his belt with a string.

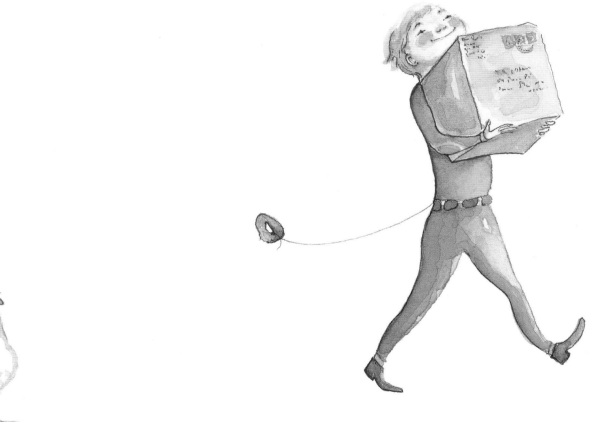

Right here and right now, things really got going,

for Daisy in knickers came galloping after.

And that brought the rest of the cast of the play,

all jumbled and tumbled with snorfles of laughter.

And so followed Mabel, their Saturday sitter,

and Adelaide Bead, who'd been doing her hair,

and a whole bunch of runners who saw all this running

and figured the race they were running went there!

Now you can imagine all the confusion

when somewhere on Main Street they picked up a band—

all noisy and joyful and jolly and gleaming,

all beaming with pleasure like this had been planned.

And soon there came others: waiters and diners,

porters with luggage, mailmen with mail,

bricklayers, horn players, painters and masons,

a heavy dirt-digger, a covey of quail.

The firemen came with their firemen's hoses.

The sign painters came with their just-painted signs.

There was a wedding reception with roses.

There was a farmer's full barnyard of swine.

And there were some things you just never saw there—
cloud catchers came with the clouds they had caught.

Citizens came from the pages of history.

Little May Pinker brought things she had thought.

And now the parade—led by one child—

had suddenly swollen to something so wild,

whirling through town so breathlessly fast

that everything shook as the Great Parade passed.

Which would have been fine—

the little town stood.

But for the parade

it didn't look good . . .

Just when their energy couldn't be topped,

right in the front, small Billy—just *stopped*.

What clucking!
And leaping!

And barking!
And giggles!

What skidding!
And bumping!

And laughing!
And snorts!

A piled-up spectacle
fit for a king!

A splashy display like the bursting of spring!

You never quite think of the marvelous things

that happen when doughnuts are tied up with strings!

And then, with one glance, small Billy departed,

leaving behind this Great Gala he'd started.

He slipped down a path to a spot in the shade,

to a place of pure cool the tallest trees made.

And all afternoon, as the bay bluely gleamed,

this Billy set sail and happily dreamed

while eating a crisp and delicious fried ring—

the doughnut he'd tied to his belt with a string.

Song of the Water Boatman and Backswimmer's Refrain

Down through the jolly waters green,
I stroke with legs both long and lean,
like a streamlined class-A submarine
...on a sunny summer's morning.
  Yo, ho, ho,
  the pond winds blow
  and upside down is the way to go.

Of plunging deep, I have no fear.
To breathe, I keep some bubbles near,
trapped on my chest in a silver sphere
...on a sunny summer's morning.
  Yo, ho, ho,
  the pond winds blow;
  beneath my wings, the air I stow.

I like to eat the dark green goo
that floats about like a veggie stew,
mixed for a water boatman true
...on a sunny summer's morning.
  Yo, ho, ho,
  the pond winds blow;
  I'd rather catch wee beasties-o.

Danger lurks in every spot—
from beetles, turtles, and their lot;
I hide down deep where the sun is not
...on a sunny summer's morning.
  Yo, ho, ho
  the pond winds blow;
  I hang up top, by the surface glow.

WATER BOATMAN, BACKSWIMMER

Common in most ponds, these two half-inch-long water bugs look almost identical. Both have boat-shaped bodies and oarlike legs. But whereas the water boatman swims right-side up, the backswimmer spends its life on its back! You can often see the backswimmer hanging belly-side up, just below the surface of the water. It is waiting for small insects to eat, while the water boatman eats mainly plant matter. Both water bugs carry bubbles of air with them to breathe, either on their bellies (primarily the water boatman) or under their wings (primarily the backswimmer).

I guess by now, it's clear to see
the boatman's life is the life for me;
among the weeds I'll always be
...on a sunny summer's morning.
   Yo, ho, ho,
   the pond winds blow;
   the backswimmer's life is the life I know!

by Joyce Sidman
illustrated by Beckie Prange

Nancy Shaw

Sheep in a Jeep

Illustrated by Margot Apple

To Allison and Danny
—N.S.

To Sue Sherman
—M.A.

Beep! Beep!

Sheep in a jeep
on a hill that's
steep.

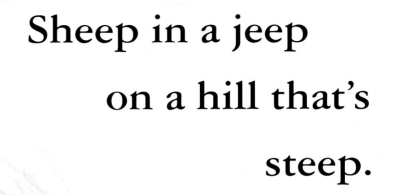

Uh-oh!

The jeep won't go.

Sheep leap
to push the jeep.

Sheep shove.
Sheep grunt.

Sheep don't think
to look up front.

Jeep goes splash!
Jeep goes thud!

Jeep goes deep
in gooey mud.

Sheep tug.

Sheep shrug.

Sheep yelp.

Sheep get help.

Jeep comes out.

Sheep shout.

Sheep cheer.

Oh, dear!

The driver sheep

forgets to steer.

Jeep in a heap.

Sheep weep.

Sheep sweep the heap.

Jeep for sale—cheap.

Tree Horse

My tree horse shakes
his rustling green mane,
arches his neck,
plunges his head down,
whinnies sharply.

His taut muscles strain.
I hold on tightly
as he rears up—
we leap into the wind,
vaulting toward sky.

by Kristine O'Connell George
illustrated by Kate Kiesler

TACKY

the Penguin

Helen Lester

Illustrated by Lynn Munsinger

There once lived a penguin.
His home was a nice icy land he shared
with his companions.

His companions were named
Goodly, Lovely, Angel, Neatly, and Perfect.

His name was Tacky.
Tacky was an odd bird.

Every day Goodly, Lovely, Angel, Neatly, and Perfect
greeted each other quietly and politely.

Tacky greeted them with a hearty slap on the back
and a loud "What's happening?"

Goodly, Lovely, Angel, Neatly, and Perfect always marched

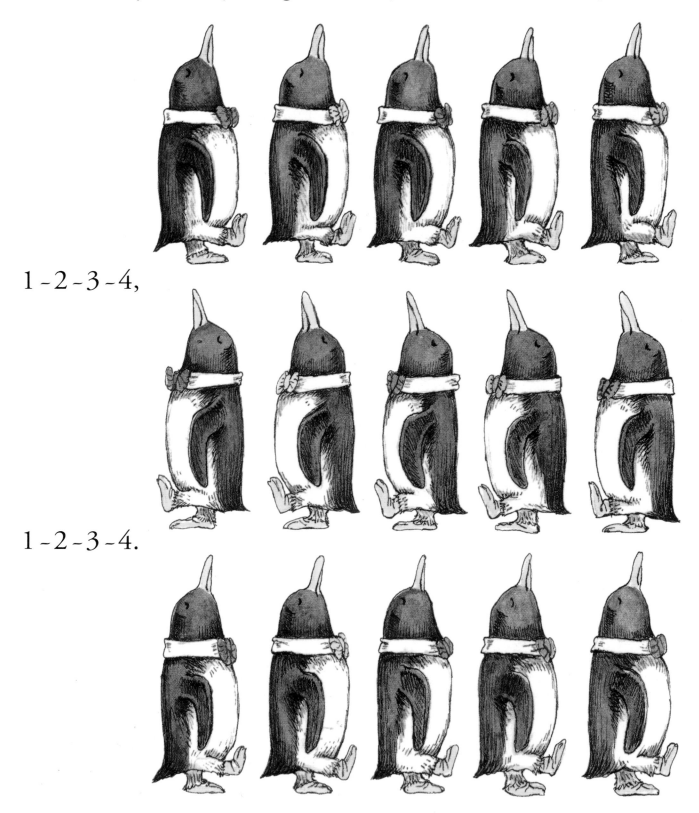

1-2-3-4,

1-2-3-4.

Tacky always marched 1-2-3,

 4-2,

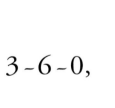

3-6-0,

 2½,

0.

His companions were graceful divers.

Tacky liked to do splashy cannonballs.

Goodly, Lovely, Angel, Neatly, and Perfect
always sang pretty songs like
"Sunrise on the Iceberg."

Tacky always sang songs like
"How Many Toes Does a Fish Have?"
Tacky was an odd bird.

One day the penguins heard the *thump...thump...thump* of feet in the distance.
This could mean only one thing.
Hunters had come.

They came with maps and traps and rocks and locks,
and they were rough and tough.
As the *thump…thump…thump*
drew closer, the penguins could hear
the growly voices chanting,

"We're gonna catch some pretty penguins,
And we'll march 'em with a switch,
And we'll sell 'em for a dollar,
And get rich, rich, RICH!"

Goodly, Lovely, Angel, Neatly, and Perfect
ran away in fright.

They hid behind a block of ice.

Tacky stood alone.

The hunters marched right up to him, chanting,

  "We're gonna catch some pretty penguins,

  And we'll march 'em with a switch,

  And we'll sell 'em for a dollar,

  And get rich, rich, RICH!"

"What's happening?" blared Tacky, giving one hunter an especially hearty slap on the back.

They growled, "We're hunting for penguins.
That's what's happening."

"PENNNNGUINS?" said Tacky. "Do you mean those birds that march neatly in a row?"
And he marched,

1 ~ 2 ~ 3,

4 ~ 2,

3 ~ 6 ~ 0,

2½,

0.

The hunters looked puzzled.

"Do you mean those birds that dive so gracefully?"
Tacky asked.

And he did a splashy cannonball.
The hunters looked wet.

"Do you mean those birds that sing such pretty songs?"
Tacky began to sing, and from behind the block of ice
came the voices of his companions,
all singing as loudly and dreadfully as they could.

"HOW MANY TOES DOES A FISH HAVE?

AND HOW MANY WINGS ON A COW?

I WONDER. YUP,

I WONDER."

The hunters could not stand the horrible singing.
This could not be the land of the pretty penguins.
They ran away with their hands clasped tightly over their ears,
leaving behind their maps and traps and rocks and locks,
and not looking at all rough and tough.

Goodly, Lovely, Angel, Neatly, and Perfect hugged Tacky.
Tacky was an odd bird but a very nice bird to have around.

Robert's
Four
At-Bats

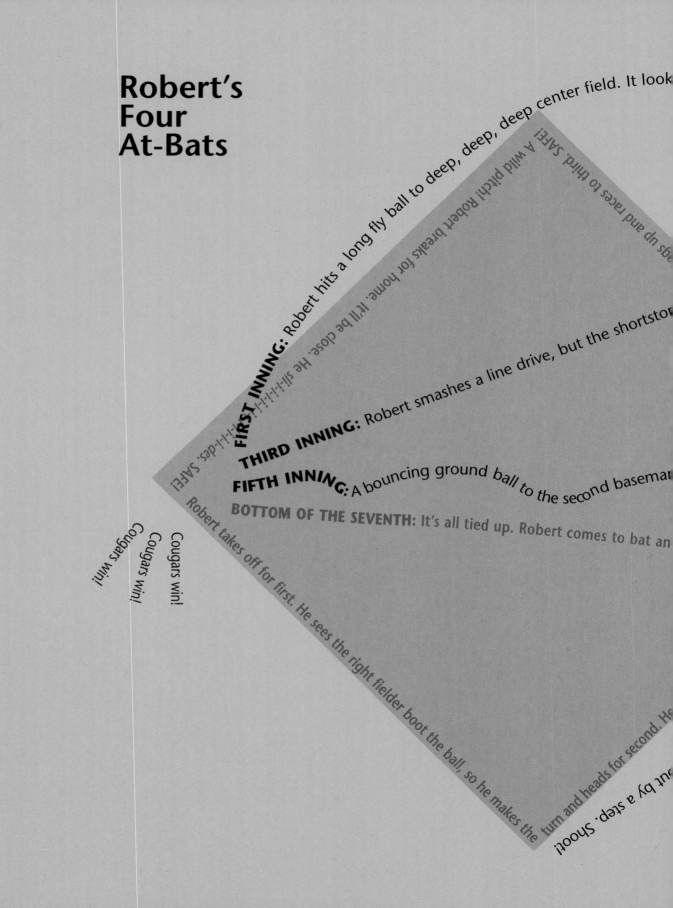

FIRST INNING: Robert hits a long fly ball to deep, deep, deep center field. It look...

THIRD INNING: Robert smashes a line drive, but the shortsto...

FIFTH INNING: A bouncing ground ball to the second basemar...

BOTTOM OF THE SEVENTH: It's all tied up. Robert comes to bat an...

A wild pitch! Robert breaks for home. He sli-i-i-i-i-i-des. SAFE!

...ags up and races to third. SAFE!

Robert takes off for first. He sees the right fielder boot the ball, so he makes the turn and heads for second. He...

...out by a step. Shoot!

Cougars win!
Cougars win!
Cougars win!

ike it might be out of here! The center fielder goes back, back, back to the fence . . . and makes the catch. Rats!

eaps and makes a fantastic grab. Darn it.

The next batter flies deep to right, Rober

t takes a wicked hop, but he snags it and fires it

ines a solid hit

can't see the ball so he sli-i-i-i-i-i-des... SAFE!

to right. The outfielder misjudges the bounce and bobbles the ball.

over to first. It's close, but Robert is

by John Grandits

Five Little Monkeys Jumping on the Bed

Retold and Illustrated by
EILEEN CHRISTELOW

EILEEN CHRISTELOW

For

Heather Morgan

Joni

Grady Stefan

——————————————————————

It was bedtime. So five little monkeys took a bath.

Five little monkeys put on their pajamas.

Five little monkeys brushed their teeth.

Five little monkeys said good night to their mama.

Then...five little monkeys jumped on the bed!

One fell off and bumped his head.

The mama called the doctor. The doctor said,

"No more monkeys jumping on the bed!"

So four little monkeys...

...jumped on the bed.

One fell off and bumped his head.

The mama called the doctor.   The doctor said,

"No more monkeys jumping on the bed!"

So three little monkeys jumped on the bed.

One fell off and bumped her head.

The mama called the doctor.

The doctor said,

"No more monkeys jumping on the bed!"

So two little monkeys jumped on the bed.

One fell off and bumped his head.

The mama called the doctor.

The doctor said,

"No more monkeys jumping on the bed!"

So one little monkey jumped on the bed.

She fell off and bumped her head.

The mama called the doctor.   The doctor said,

"NO MORE MONKEYS JUMPING ON THE BED!"

So five little monkeys fell fast asleep.

"Thank goodness!" said the mama.

"Now I can go to bed!"

THE SPHINX
AIN'T ALL THAT—

YEAH, YOU HEARD ME

I'm just saying, the Sphinx ain't as great as she thinks.

Her Egyptian hat thing is all covered in bling, and she has a nice face, but I'll cut to the chase:

From her neck to her *butt*, she don't look like King Tut.

And
because
of the Sphinx,
all of Egypt now stinks.
You can follow your nose
to the places she goes:
in the Nile, on a pyramid, *anywhere* here amid
all of the sand of her litter-box land.

While you're cleaning her mess, she'll invite you to guess:

What has four legs at dawn
only two later on,
and then three legs at night?*

She'll just yawn if you're right;
if you're *not* good at riddles,
then you're
Tender
Vittles.

by Adam Rex

* The answer to the Riddle of the Sphinx is man: He crawls on all fours at the beginning of his life, walks on two legs later on, and uses a cane as a third leg in his old age.

MIKE MULLIGAN
AND HIS
STEAM SHOVEL

STORY AND PICTURES BY VIRGINIA LEE BURTON

TO

MIKE

Mike Mulligan had a steam shovel,
a beautiful red steam shovel.
Her name was Mary Anne.
Mike Mulligan was very proud of Mary Anne.
He always said that she could dig as much in a day
as a hundred men could dig in a week,
but he had never been quite sure
that this was true.

Mike Mulligan and Mary Anne
had been digging together
for years and years.
Mike Mulligan took such good care
of Mary Anne
she never grew old.

It was Mike Mulligan and Mary Anne
    and some others
    who dug the great canals
    for the big boats
    to sail through.

It was Mike Mulligan
and Mary Anne
and some others
who cut through
the high mountains
so that trains
could go through.

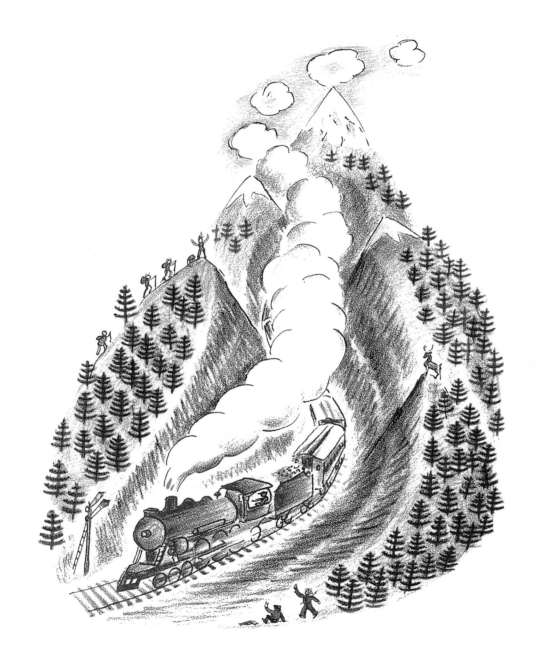

It was Mike Mulligan and Mary Anne
and some others
who lowered the hills
and straightened the curves

to make the long highways
for the automobiles.

It was Mike Mulligan
and Mary Anne
and some others
who smoothed out the ground
and filled in the holes

to make landing fields
for the airplanes.

And it was Mike Mulligan
and Mary Anne
and some others
who dug the deep holes
for the cellars
of the tall skyscrapers
in the big cities.
When people used to stop
and watch them,
Mike Mulligan and Mary Anne
used to dig a little faster
and a little better.
The more people stopped,
the faster and better they dug.
Some days they would keep
as many as thirty-seven trucks
busy taking away the dirt they had dug.

Then along came
   the new gasoline shovels
     and the new electric shovels
      and the new Diesel motor shovels
        and took all the jobs away from the steam shovels.

Mike Mulligan

and Mary Anne

were

VERY

SAD.

All the other steam shovels were being sold for junk,
or left out in old gravel pits to rust and fall apart.
Mike loved Mary Anne. He couldn't do that to her.

He had taken
such good care of her
that she could still dig
as much in a day
as a hundred men
could dig in a week;
at least he thought she could
but he wasn't quite sure.
Everywhere they went
the new gas shovels
and the new electric shovels
and the new Diesel motor shovels
had all the jobs. No one wanted
Mike Mulligan and Mary Anne anymore.
Then one day Mike read in a newspaper that the town
of Popperville was going to build a new town hall.
"We are going to dig the cellar of that town hall,"
said Mike to Mary Anne, and off they started.

They left the canals
  and the railroads
    and the highways
     and the airports
      and the big cities
        where no one wanted them anymore
        and went away out in the country.

They crawled along slowly
up the hills and down the hills
till they came to the little town
of Popperville.

When they got there they found that the selectmen
were just deciding who should dig the cellar for the new town hall.
Mike Mulligan spoke to Henry B. Swap, one of the selectmen.
"I heard," he said, "that you are going
to build a new town hall. Mary Anne and I
will dig the cellar for you in just one day."
"What!" said Henry B. Swap. "Dig a cellar in a day!
It would take a hundred men at least a week
to dig the cellar for our new town hall."
"Sure," said Mike, "but Mary Anne can dig as much in a day
as a hundred men can dig in a week."
Though he had never been quite sure that this was true.
Then he added,
"If we can't do it, you won't have to pay."
Henry B. Swap thought that this would be
an easy way to get part of the cellar dug for nothing,
so he smiled in rather a mean way
and gave the job of digging the cellar of the new town hall
to Mike Mulligan and Mary Anne.

They started in
early the next morning.
Soon a little boy came along.
"Do you think you will finish by sundown?"
he said to Mike Mulligan.
"Sure," said Mike, "if you stay and watch us.
We always work faster and better
when someone is watching us."
So the little boy stayed to watch.

Then Mrs. McGillicuddy,
Henry B. Swap,
and the Town Constable
came over to see
what was happening,
and they stayed to watch.

Mike Mulligan
and Mary Anne
dug a little faster
and a little better.

This gave the little boy a good idea.
He ran off and told the postman with the morning mail,
the telegraph boy on his bicycle,
the milkman with his cart and horse,
the doctor on his way home,
and the farmer and his family
coming into town for the day,
and they stopped and stayed to watch.
That made Mike Mulligan and Mary Anne
dig a little faster and a little better.
They finished the first corner
neat and square . . .
but the sun was getting higher.

Clang! Clang! Clang!
The Fire Department arrived.
They had seen the smoke
and thought there was a fire.
Then the little boy said,
"Why don't you stay and watch?"
So the Fire Department of Popperville
stayed to watch Mike Mulligan and Mary Anne.
When they heard the fire engine, the children
in the school across the street couldn't keep
their eyes on their lessons. The teacher called
a long recess and the whole school came out to watch.
That made Mike Mulligan and Mary Anne
dig still faster and still better.

They finished the second corner neat and square,
but the sun was right up in the top of the sky.

Now the girl who answers
the telephone called up the next towns
of Bangerville and Bopperville and
Kipperville and Kopperville and told them
what was happening in Popperville.
All the people came over to see
if Mike Mulligan and his steam shovel
could dig the cellar in just one day.
The more people came, the faster
Mike Mulligan and Mary Anne dug.
But they would have to hurry.
They were only halfway through
and the sun was beginning to go down.

They finished the third corner . . . neat and square.

269

Never had Mike Mulligan and Mary Anne
had so many people to watch them;
never had they dug so fast and so well;
and never had the sun seemed
to go down so fast.
"Hurry, Mike Mulligan!
  Hurry! Hurry!"
    shouted the little boy.
      "There's not much more time!"
        Dirt was flying everywhere,
          and the smoke and steam were so thick
            that the people could hardly see anything.
              But listen!

BING! BANG! CRASH! SLAM!
LOUDER AND LOUDER,
FASTER AND
FASTER.

Then suddenly it was quiet.
Slowly the dirt settled down.
The smoke and steam cleared away,
and there was the cellar,
all finished.

Four corners . . . neat and square;
four walls . . . straight down,
and Mike Mulligan and Mary Anne at the bottom,
and the sun was just going down behind the hill.
"Hurray!" shouted the people. "Hurray for Mike Mulligan
and his steam shovel! They have dug the cellar in just one day!"

Suddenly the little boy said,
"How are they going to get out?"
"That's right," said Mrs. McGillicuddy
to Henry B. Swap. "How is he going
to get his steam shovel out?"
Henry B. Swap didn't answer,
but he smiled in a rather mean way.
Then everybody said,
"How are they going to get out?
"Hi! Mike Mulligan!
How are you going to get
your steam shovel out?"

Mike Mulligan
looked around
at the four square walls
and four square corners,
and he said,
"We've dug so fast
and we've dug so well
that we've quite forgotten
to leave a way out!"
Nothing like this had ever happened
to Mike Mulligan and Mary Anne before,
and they didn't know what to do.

Nothing like this
      had ever happened before
        in Popperville.
      Everybody started
    talking at once,
        and everybody had
          a different idea,
          and everybody thought
      that his idea was the best.
They talked and they talked
        and they argued and they fought
          till they were worn out,
          and still no one knew how to get
          Mike Mulligan and Mary Anne
          out of the cellar they had dug.
        Then Henry B. Swap said,
      "The job isn't finished because
      Mary Anne isn't out of the cellar,
    so Mike Mulligan won't get paid."
And he smiled again in a rather mean way.

Now the little boy,
who had been keeping very quiet,
had another good idea.
He said,
"Why couldn't we leave Mary Anne in the cellar
and build the new town hall above her?
Let her be the furnace for the new town hall*
and let Mike Mulligan be the janitor.
Then you wouldn't have to buy a new furnace,
and we could pay Mike Mulligan
for digging the cellar
in just one day."

* Acknowledgments to Dickie Birkenbush.

"Why not?" said Henry B. Swap,
   and smiled in a way
     that was not quite so mean.
       "Why not?" said Mrs. McGillicuddy.
       "Why not?" said the Town Constable.
       "Why not?" said all the people.
       So they found a ladder
         and climbed down into the cellar
           to ask Mike Mulligan and Mary Anne.

"Why not?" said Mike Mulligan.
So it was decided,
   and everybody was happy.

They built the new town hall
right over Mike Mulligan and Mary Anne.
It was finished before winter.

Every day the little boy goes over to see
Mike Mulligan and Mary Anne,
and Mrs. McGillicuddy takes him
nice hot apple pies. As for Henry B. Swap,
he spends most of his time in the cellar
of the new town hall listening to the stories
that Mike Mulligan has to tell
and smiling in a way that isn't mean at all.

Now when you go to Popperville,
be sure to go down in the cellar
    of the new town hall.
    There they'll be,
        Mike Mulligan and Mary Anne . . .
        Mike in his rocking chair
            smoking his pipe,
            and Mary Anne beside him,
                warming up the meetings
                in the new town hall.

Lying on the lawn,
we study the blackboard sky,
connecting the dots.

by Bob Raczka
illustrated by Peter H. Reynolds

Meet the Authors and Illustrators

H. A. AND MARGRET REY

HANS AUGUSTO REY and MARGRET REY escaped Nazi-occupied Paris in 1940 by bicycle, carrying the manuscript for the first book about Curious George. They came to live in the United States, and *Curious George* was published in 1941. You can learn more about the Reys and Curious George, and access games, activities, downloads, and PBS television shows at www.curiousgeorge.com.

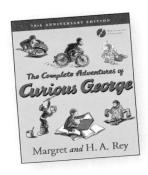

BERNARD WABER AND PAULIS WABER

BERNARD WABER is the beloved, best-selling author and illustrator of eight books about everyone's favorite crocodile, Lyle. He lives in Baldwin Harbor, New York.

PAULIS WABER is the illustrator of *Lyle Walks the Dogs* and the daughter of Bernard Waber. She lives with her husband and three children in Washington, D.C. The first book about Lyle, 1962's *The House on East 88th Street*, was dedicated to her.

You can learn more about the Wabers, Lyle, and other wonderful books at waberchat.workpress.com.

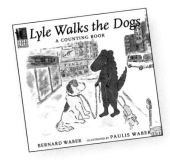

SUSAN MEDDAUGH

Susan Meddaugh is the author and illustrator of the beloved Martha Speaks series. She lives in Sherborn, Massachusetts, with her son and three shelter dogs. Meddaugh's real dog named Martha inspired six picture books, a PBS television series, and many books based on the show. Visit pbskids.org/martha/ to find out more about Susan Meddaugh and Martha, and to access games, downloads, videos, and more.

NIKKI GRIMES AND JAVAKA STEPTOE

Nikki Grimes lives in California and has written more than two dozen books for children, including two Coretta Scott King Honor books, *Jazmin's Notebook* and *Meet Danitra Brown.*

Javaka Steptoe is the illustrator of the poetry anthology, *In Daddy's Arms I Am Tall,* which won the Coretta Scott King Award for Illustration, and of *Jimi: Sounds Like a Rainbow, A Story of Young Jimi Hendrix,* which was a Coretta Scott King Honor Award winner. He lives in Brooklyn, New York.

To find out more, visit www.nikkigrimes.com to find blog posts, news, and audio of Nikki Grimes reading her work; and visit www.javaka.com to learn more about Javaka Steptoe's books and artwork.

HELEN LESTER AND LYNN MUNSINGER

Helen Lester is a full-time writer who makes her home in Pawling, New York. She has written numerous books featuring everyone's favorite penguin, Tacky, and lots of other memorable characters, often with the illustrator Lynn Munsinger.

Lynn Munsinger is a full-time illustrator who created the Tacky the Penguin series with Helen Lester. They have made more than twenty-five fantastic books together, including *A Porcupine Named Fluffy* and *Hooway for Wodney Wat.* Munsinger divides her time between Connecticut and Vermont.

To find out more about Tacky, see photos, read interviews, and more, visit www.helenlester.com.

EILEEN CHRISTELOW

Eileen Christelow has written and illustrated many fun and funny picture books, including the Five Little Monkeys series, *Vote!,* and *Letters from a Desperate Dog.* She and her husband, Ahren, live in Vermont.

For more information about the Five Little Monkeys, fun activities, information on how illustrations are created, and comic strips, visit www.christelow.com.

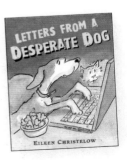

NANCY SHAW AND MARGOT APPLE

NANCY SHAW is the author of seven beloved tales featuring the endearing and comical sheep, an idea born during a very long car trip with her husband and two children. She lives in Ann Arbor, Michigan, with her family.

MARGOT APPLE has illustrated more than fifty books for children, including all seven books about the bumbling sheep, and has also produced illustrations for *Cricket* and *Ladybug* magazines. She now lives in Shelburn Falls, Massachusetts, with her husband and pets.

For more about the Sheep and their adventures and to access fun activities, be sure to visit www.nancyshawbooks.com.

KRISTINE O'CONNELL GEORGE AND KATE KIESLER

KRISTINE O'CONNELL GEORGE's many volumes of poetry for children have received numerous honors, including the Lee Bennett Hopkins Poetry Award, International Reading Association / Lee Bennett Hopkins Promising Poet Award, the Myra Cohn Livingston Poetry Award, and the Claudia Lewis Poetry Award.

KATE KIESLER is a fine artist and illustrator who has created art for more than twenty books for children including *Crab Moon* by Ruth Horowitz and *The Great Frog Race* by Kristine O'Connell George. She lives in Colorado, the landscape of which inspires much of her painting.

For more about Kristine O'Connell George's books, and to find activities for teachers and children and read-aloud audio clips, visit www.kristinegeorge.com.

 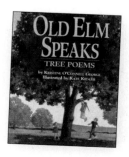

REBECCA BOND

REBECCA BOND is the author of several superb picture books, including *The Great Doughnut Parade* and *In the Belly of an Ox.* She grew up in the tiny village of Peacham, Vermont, and now works as a book designer and lives in Jamaica Plain, Massachusetts.

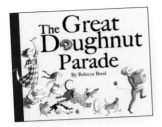 

VIRGINIA LEE BURTON

VIRGINIA LEE BURTON (1909–1968) was the award-winning author and illustrator of some of the most enduring children's books ever written, including *Mike Mulligan and His Steam Shovel, Katy and the Big Snow,* and *The Little House,* which won the Caldecott Medal in 1943.

DOUGLAS FLORIAN

DOUGLAS FLORIAN is the creator of many acclaimed poetic picture books, including *Zoo's Who; Bow Wow Meow Meow; Lizards, Frogs, and Polliwogs; Mammalabilia; Insectlopedia;* and *Omnibeasts.* He lives and works in New York City. Visit him at floriancafe.blogspot.com.

CALEF BROWN

Calef Brown is an artist, a writer, and frequently a blue elephant. Brown's illustrations have appeared in many magazines and newspapers, and his paintings have been exhibited in N.Y., L.A., S.F., and other places without fancy initials, such as Osaka and Rome. His books for Houghton Mifflin Harcourt include the successful *Polkabats and Octopus Slacks, Dutch Sneakers and Flea Keepers,* and *Flamingos on the Roof.* He lives in Maine, and you can learn more about his books, poetry, and artwork at www.calefbrown.com.

JOYCE SIDMAN AND BECKIE PRANGE

Joyce Sidman is the award-winning poet of *Song of the Water Boatman, Red Sings from Treetops,* and *Dark Emperor and Other Poems of the Night,* a Newbery Honor book. She has won both the Lee Bennet Hopkins Award and Bank Street's Claudia Lewis Award for her poetry. Sidman says, "For me, writing is a matter of finding what things amaze and intrigue me and what things give me joy." She lives in Wayzata, Minnesota.

Beckie Prange lives in Ely, Minnesota, where she spends as much time as possible in the woods looking at lichens, crows, and other hardy northern species. *Song of the Water Boatman* was her first book, and she received a Caldecott Honor for its illustrations.

For more information about *Song of the Water Boatman,* as well as to access tips for writers, poetry kits for teachers, poetry writing prompts, and more, visit www.joycesidman.com. And for a further window into the fine art of woodcutting, visit www.beckieprange.com.

ADAM REX

ADAM REX is the author and illustrator of *PSSST!, Tree Ring Circus, Frankenstein Takes the Cake*, and the *New York Times* bestseller *Frankenstein Makes a Sandwich*. He lives in Philadelphia, Pennsylvania. Visit his website at www.adamrex.com for more information about his books, and to find news, a blog, artwork, and more.

BOB RACZKA AND PETER REYNOLDS

BOB RACZKA lives with his wife, sons, daughter, and dog, Rufus, in Glen Ellyn, Illinois. He is the author of several children's books, but *Guyku* is his first with Houghton Mifflin Harcourt. Raczka's favorite guy things include art, baseball, books, golf, grilling, and poetry.

PETER H. REYNOLDS is a *New York Times* best-selling illustrator who has created many acclaimed books for children, including *The Dot, Ish,* and *The North Star.* His Massachusetts bookstore, The Blue Bunny, and his company, FableVision, are dedicated to sharing "stories that matter, stories that move."

To find out more, visit www.bobraczka.com; and to access blogs, news, tips for writers, and artwork, visit www.peterhreynolds.com.

JOHN GRANDITS

JOHN GRANDITS is an acclaimed book and magazine designer and the author of *Technically, It's Not My Fault* and *Blue Lipstick,* award-winning books of concrete poetry, as well as *The Travel Game.* He lives in Red Bank, New Jersey, with his wife, Joanne, a children's librarian, and Gilbert, an evil cat. Learn more about his books, read the poem of the month, and find out more about concrete poetry at www.johngrandits.com.

All rights reserved. For information about permission to reproduce selections from this book, write to Permissions, Houghton Mifflin Harcourt Publishing Company, 215 Park Avenue South, New York, New York 10003.

Published in the United States by Houghton Mifflin Harcourt Publishing Company.

www.hmhbooks.com

Manufactured in China
LEO 10 9 8 7 6 5 4 3 2 1
4500289936

Curious George and the Firefighters
Copyright © 2004 by Houghton Mifflin Company

Lyle Walks the Dogs
Text copyright © 2010 by Bernard Waber
Illustrations copyright © 2010 by Paulis Waber

Martha Speaks
Copyright © 1992 by Susan Meddaugh

The Great Doughnut Parade
Copyright © 2007 by Rebecca Bond

Sheep in a Jeep
Text copyright © 1986 by Nancy Shaw

Illustrations copyright © 1986 by Margot Apple

Tacky the Penguin
Text copyright © 1988 by Helen Lester
Illustrations copyright © 1988 by Lynn Munsinger

Five Little Monkeys Jumping on the Bed
Copyright © 1989 by Eileen Christelow

Mike Mulligan and His Steam Shovel
Copyright © 1939 by Virginia Lee Demetrios
Copyright © renewed 1967 by Aristides Burton Demetrios and Michael Burton Demetrios

"The Cheetah"
from *Bow Wow Meow Meow* copyright © 2003 by Douglas Florian

"The Egret"
from *Soup for Breakfast* copyright © 2008 by Calef Brown

"Caterpillar"
from *A Pocketful of Poems*
Text copyright © 2001 by Nikki Grimes
Illustrations copyright © 2001 by Javaka Steptoe

"Song of the Water Boatman"
from *Song of the Water Boatman*
Text copyright © 2005 by Joyce Sidman
Illustrations copyright © 2005 by Beckie Prange

"Tree Horse"
from *Old Elm Speaks: Tree Poems*
Text copyright © 1998 by Kristine O'Connell George
Illustrations copyright © 1998 by Kate Kiesler

"Robert's Four At-Bats"
from *Techincally, It's Not My Fault*
copyright © 2004 by John Grandits

"The Sphinx Ain't All That"
from *Frankenstein Takes the Cake*
copyright © 2008 by Adam Rex

"Lying on the Lawn"
from *Guyku*
Text copyright © 2010 by Bob Raczka
Illustrations copyright © 2010 by Peter H. Reynolds